Tease Me

A Possessive Billionaire Workplace Romance

Billionaire Boy's Club
Book 1

KeKe Renée

304 Publishing Company

 Created with Vellum

Latest Releases by Keke Renée:

- Wet Heat (Wet Heat Series Book 1)
- Every Time We Touch Novelette (Wet Heat Book 2 Series)
- His Peace, Her Pleasure
- Baby, It's Cold Outside
- Love Don't Live Here Anymore, Vanessa Andrew Book 1
- Love Don't Live Here Anymore, Isabella Andrew Book 2
- One Night Only—A Novelette (Love by Design Book 1)
- Cassian and Savannah (Love by Design Book 2)
- Deidra's Love (Love by Design Book 3)
- Protecting Bria (Special Force Operation Alphas)
- Sensual: A Brother's Best Friend Romance
- Seek To Please Book 1
- Seek To Touch Book 2
- Seek To Bare Book 3
- Seek To Love Book 4

Disclaimer

THIS WORK OF FICTION contains strong language and explicit sexual content and is only intended for mature readers. This story contains unconventional situations, language, and sexual encounters that may offend some readers. This book is for mature readers (18+).

I WANT TO THANK FIRST my readers for loving these characters so much and waiting so long for them to come back.

Acknowledgments

I CAN'T MENTION ENOUGH the support and dedication of my author buddies for keeping me uplifted. My behind-the-scenes team of beta readers, editors, designers, and more. As a writer, I continue to strive for the best, and I appreciate everyone who reads my work. Without your continual feedback, I wouldn't be on this path, letting doubts slip away.

Introduction

Are you signed up for my newsletter?

Join today for all the latest new releases, contests, giveaways, sneak peeks, and more.

https://BookHip.com/BKRPJL

Synopsis

Money and power, I understand. This exquisite beauty is a mystery.

From the first moment she walked into my club, I was mesmerized by her. I had to claim her at first sight. My body demanded it.

But Sanya knows how to seduce, tease, and beguile me.

Now I want more than just a fling.

Can I convince her that my playboy days are behind me?

Indulge in seduction in this new series from KeKe Renée. During the day, these billionaires are powerful tycoons who run the city, but at night, they come to Billionaire Boys Club to play.

Chapter 1

Gerald

Friday

My scowl didn't deter my assistant one bit. She knew I hated it when these events were planned at my place of business. I built it as an escape for my friends and their associates to unwind after a long work day. Being a well-known businessman in Seattle and having people in my face non-stop itched at my brain.

Melinda blinked those big brown eyes. "Mr. Barlowe, it will only be for one night."

I couldn't say no if I wanted to because she'd been my lifesaver. Scrubbing a hand down my face, I attempted to be a little less annoyed. "You want to hold a book club meeting at my cigar bar on Sunday. Am I hearing you right?"

She nodded hesitantly. "Before you say no, think about what it could do for business."

"My business is fine."

"It's my turn to host the book club meeting, and I told my friends we could do it here."

I grunted and sat up in my chair. "So you lied."

"I promise to clean up afterward."

Melinda was one of the most loyal people I'd ever met. She was like an annoying little sister.

"Besides, Sanya will help keep it down." Melinda grinned and slipped the flyer on my desk.

"Sanya?"

"I asked her if she would help me close up that night before coming to talk with you."

"Bring her in here."

"She's working the floor."

"I don't care."

"Please don't fight with her." Melinda groaned.

I pressed the button on the intercom to the bar.

"Yes, Mr. Barlowe."

Sanya's lack of enthusiasm made me laugh. "Sanya, come to my office."

"I'm working."

"Put someone else on the bar."

I heard her loud sigh and waited for her smart-mouth reply. "May I ask why I'm needed in your office?"

"Sanya, I told him about the book club," Melinda said, interrupting my response.

Glaring at her, I pointed my finger to be quiet. "Come to my office now."

"Yes, sir," Sanya replied.

Her reply reminded me of our last time together, which she'd avoided discussing. I turned to Melinda. "You can go."

She pouted. "But what about my book club?"

A tap on the door was preceded by Sanya entering the room. She wore the Billionaire Boys Club uniform of thigh-high stockings with a garter belt and crop top with the business logo woven in gold. She was tall at five-eight, with warm-brown skin and curves in all the right places.

Melinda hopped up and gave me a hard stare. "Sorry, Sanya. He's not in a friendly mood today." She stomped out of my office, closing the door behind her.

I lounged in my chair, staring at Sanya, who avoided eye contact. "Take a seat."

"No."

"I said, take a seat."

Frowning, Sanya sat on the couch away from my desk.

"You're too far away."

"I like it over here."

"Why must you play these games?"

"Games?" Sanya jumped up, marched to my desk, and got in my face.

I grabbed her wrist and pulled her into my lap, nuzzling my face into her neck.

"Gerald, no," Sanya moaned as I ran a hand up her thigh.

"I missed you."

"We decided one time only."

"*You* decided. I didn't."

The day Sanya walked in, I'd stood off in the back as Troy interviewed her so I could see how she conducted herself. My place wasn't a low-brow bar or strip club for men to ogle at women. I'd built a high-end establishment where men could relax and talk with other like-minded people. An exclusive men-only club where you had to value discretion and pay in the range of a half million dollars for membership. Certain deals were born in Billionaire Boys Club, and having the details getting out would hurt the credibility of the club, especially when politics were involved.

Sanya came in with confidence, boldness, and a sex appeal I knew would entice every man who saw her beauty. Which was why I only let her work the bar and tend to me, although she was still paid the same as the other women.

She was pissed with me now because I'd told her not to work at other parties after our one night together. Usually, I slept with a woman and moved on, but Sanya made me want more.

"How are we supposed to be professional at work if you're taking jobs from me?"

Nibbling her neck, I brush my fingers across her shoulder and down her arm. "Fuck, who cares what's professional?"

"Gerald, I want to continue working here, but you need to control yourself."

Her words made me freeze, and I pulled back to stare into her eyes. "What are you saying?" I held her in place as she tried to escape my lap.

"I could quit and work somewhere else."

"Like where?" I wanted to know who had the balls to approach my employees with offers to work elsewhere.

"None of your business." Sanya climbed out of my lap.

"Sanya."

"I'm not a toy," she snarled, hovering over my desk.

I sighed heavily. "Here we go."

She threw up her hands. "You're doing it again."

"What? Making sure my investments stay where they belong." I stood and slipped my hands into my pockets.

"Trying to control me. I came here to work, and you've made it pretty clear what you think of me."

I slammed my hand on the desk. "That's bullshit!"

The door opened, and Melinda glanced between Sanya and me. "Mr. Barlowe, I have Senator Ayton on line three."

"We'll discuss this later, Sanya."

"I think we're both clear. No further discussion is needed. Melinda asked me to help with the book club unless you have any rejections." Sanya hiked a brow, waiting for me to disagree in front of Melinda.

I nodded to keep the peace. "Melinda, you can have your book club, and Sanya would be happy to help."

I waited for the door to close behind them before taking a deep breath and pausing to get my head together. Sanya's spiciness meant something was bothering her. She'd avoided being alone with me, and her flushed beige cheeks had shown she'd been ready to explode. Usually, she lit up a room with her presence, but she was off today. She seemed down and uninterested in dealing with my shit.

I grabbed the phone to take the call. "Senator, how are you?"

"Hey, Gerald. Feeling good. When's the next game? I'm eager to beat your ass again," Senator Remington Ayton chuckled.

I smirked. "I seem to recall you lost at poker, my friend."

"That's because I was drinking too many of those damn shots you kept placing in front of us." Remington huffed.

I shrugged. "Not my fault you can't handle your liquor."

"Fuck you, G."

Taunting him was always fun. Our friendship went back to our college days. Remington had been a playboy with a string of women pining for him. Coming from a small town in Seattle, my parents were delighted when I made friends in college. Remington had been the popular jock in a college town where the guys competed to be the top dog on campus. He hadn't let his ego get in the way of our friendship, even when I got us into brawls at the bar. My cockiness always got me into trouble, but it paid off in the long run when I got my business degree and invented income streams in the tech world.

"You ready to lose more money to me?" I taunted.

"Not going to happen," Remington scoffed.

"I reserved the place for tonight. Bring my money and leave your whining at home."

"We'll see. I wanted to talk to you about something that has the potential to be incredibly good or incredibly bad."

"Interesting statement. You don't do simple, huh?"

"Our business is never simple."

"Says the senator who can have anything he wants."

"Comes with a cost, my friend."

Chapter 2

Sanya

A year ago...

Parking my car, I checked my makeup and fixed my curls. My goal today was to get this job and save to start my own business one day. Locking my doors, I sauntered to the door, and the guard let me inside.

I pushed all thoughts from my head and prepared to interview for the open cocktail server position at Billionaire Boys Club. I headed for the square booth in the corner where two people were sitting, a woman and a man.

"Sanya, right?" The guy rose to shake my hand.

"Yes. Are you Troy?"

"Yep, and this is Melinda."

I nodded at Melinda. "Nice to meet you."

"You too. Thanks for coming down. I know you've been waiting to hear from us."

"No problem. I figured you were busy."

Scanning the room, I noticed a man standing in the back corner near the bar. There was something different about him that made my heart beat faster and my palms sweat.

"

"Are you available to start?" Melinda asked.

I blinked. "I'm sorry. What did you say?"

Troy smiled. "We don't need to move forward with the interview."

"What about—"

He held up his hand to stall me. "You're hired. When can you start?"

My mouth dropped open. I hadn't expected to be offered the job on the spot. "Um, tomorrow?"

I took a deep breath as I slammed the bottle on the counter. Gerald had always been able to push my buttons, and I'd been regretting working here for the last year. If it weren't for the money I made, I'd quit, find a new line of work and focus on traveling and my family.

Melinda stood next to me, rubbing my back. "Gerald means well."

"He's a dick."

"He's your dick," Melinda joked.

I slapped her arm for bringing up the secret I'd told her never to discuss in public.

"Sorry." Melinda giggled, picking up the bottle of tequila and placing it back in the right spot.

"It was a one-time thing."

"Who are you trying to convince? Me or you?" Melinda asked, motioning between us.

"Hey, Sanya. Can I get two Hennessy's on the rocks?" one of the other bottle girls asked, approaching the bar and holding out her order.

"Sure, give me a minute, Cariss."

"What's going on?" Cariss questioned.

"Guy problems," Melinda replied.

I glared at her for talking to Cariss, of all people.

"Really? Who are we talking about?"

"Nobody," I said and hurriedly fixed her drinks.

I pasted on a smile, but Cariss and I weren't friends. Hell, we were barely civil. Cariss would use it against me if I revealed that I'd fallen for the boss. Melinda had told me that Cariss acted like the Queen of the club and expected everybody to bow down to her. Anytime she came at me with bullshit, I gave it right back to her with a smile.

The two guys I'm serving have piqued my interest." Cariss said, waving over her shoulder at the two men staring at us.

Working at an elite club like Billionaire Boys Club made every guy think the women would sleep with them for money. Cariss would gladly take each one if she could. My goal was to keep things professional. Well, it was until a few weeks ago when I finally gave in to my desire and slept with Gerald.

I'd been closing up with another girl and told her she could leave to catch a late-night movie with her boyfriend. Gerald was usually gone earlier in the day, but he'd been working late that night when I stopped by his office to drop off some papers.

Knowing we were alone, the attraction we'd been dancing around had exploded in a heated kiss, and one thing led to another. But he was my boss. I couldn't forget that.

"Really, Melinda? You know what Cariss is like." I huffed once Cariss had returned to her table with the drinks.

Melinda grimaced. "Sorry. I wasn't thinking."

"I'm already regretting helping you with the book

club."

She grinned and stretched her arm around my shoulder like she always did to get on my good side. "You wouldn't let your friend down,"

"What book are you reading this week?"

"It's a toss-up between Before I Let Go by Kennedy Ryan or Elio by L.K. Ryan."

I nodded. "Both sound good."

"How are you doing with the business end?"

"Researching any open positions. I want to talk to Gerald about any upcoming openings in any of his businesses, but I doubt he'd tell me."

"I can look into it for you."

"Thanks, Melinda. You know how arrogant he can be."

"Your dream is to start a premier management company, and you will."

"Friend, you're the best. Are you hungry?"

"No. I need to get back to work before the grumpy man comes out." Melinda giggled.

"Yeah, the doors will open soon, and I need to start preparing the bar."

Melinda hugged me before heading back to her office. I added more supplies to the order and set up the bar ready for tonight.

Chapter 3

Gerald

Sunday

I unlocked the door to my club and strolled inside. As I headed to the office to retrieve some papers, I heard laughter from the cigar bar.

"What the fuck?" I muttered.

A group of women were sitting around a long table covered with books and holding drinks. My eyes fell on the one woman I couldn't stay away from.

"Mr. Barlowe! What are you doing here?" Melinda asked.

"I forgot some papers."

"Oh."

"How are you ladies doing?"

"Fine," they all chorused.

"Sanya, can I speak to you in my office?"

"Why?" She held my gaze unflinchingly.

Not backing down, I moved around the table and bent to whisper in her ear. "Come to my office, or I'll eat your pussy in front of everyone." I kissed the sensitive spot behind her ear.

Plopping her napkin on the table, she slid the chair back and stood. "Give me a minute, ladies."

"Girl, take your time," one of the women said, and the others chuckled at her response.

I tried to take her hand, but she snatched it from my grip.

"Melinda told me you're looking for another job," I said as I closed my office door behind us.

Sanya rounded on me. "Melinda did what?"

"Calm down. She said you're interested in management, and it just so happens I have a position open."

"No." Sanya headed for the door.

I stepped in front of her. "Baby, I have the means and need the help."

"You're only looking to keep me because of what we did a few weeks ago."

"Do you honestly think sex is the main reason?" Moving closer, I dip my head and nip at her lips. She moaned but tried to pull back. "Stop fighting us."

"Working together wouldn't be good."

"You already work for me."

"You're missing the point."

I moved my hands down to her ass, grabbing her plump cheeks. "Look me in the eye and tell me you regret what we did."

Sanya pushed me away and almost ran from the office.

* * *

I stepped to the side as I opened the front door of my condo.

Sanya strolled inside with a frown. "We've almost gotten caught too many times, Gerald."

I shrugged. "Who cares?"

She waved her finger in my face. "I do. This is the last time you call me to your home."

"Take off your coat."

"I'm not staying."

"Yes, you are, darling."

I grasped her neck from behind, and her soft gasp revealed that I wasn't alone in my feelings. I slipped my hand around her waist and nuzzled behind her ear.

"Gerald," she moaned, reaching around to cup my head.

"Take off your coat, Sanya."

"We can't, Gerald." Sanya turned, her hands gripping my shoulders.

I tilted her head up and captured her lips. "Yes, we can, baby." I slid my hands down her hips and grabbed her ass as I slipped my tongue inside her mouth.

"Mmmm..."

I pulled back to look at her. "Are you going to take the jacket off, or should I?"

She nodded, and I lifted her in my arms, carrying her to my bedroom. I set her on her feet, and our gazes met and held as we undressed.

"I missed you," I muttered as I sat on the bed and tugged her toward me.

She straddled my lap. "I thought about your question the other day."

"Oh?"

"Becoming the manager at the club."

"Sanya."

"Seriously, we have too much tension between us. We'd never get any work done."

"Think about it some more." I nibbled on her neck and gently bit her earlobe.

Sliding my hand in the waist of her panties, I ripped them off and eased a finger into her wet heat. I stoked her in maddening circles, stopping before she came.

"Stop playing with me," Sanya gasped, tugging at my hair and grinding in my lap.

"I like to tease you."

I tossed her on the bed, shouldered her legs open, and buried my head between her thighs. I speared my tongue inside her, moving it in and out and lingering around her nub. I wanted to feel her convulsing and creaming around me.

I crawled up her body, seeing the lust in her eyes. She grabbed my hard dick and coated it with her juices. Our eyes locked as I pushed forward, sinking deep inside her.

"Baby," I huffed, trying to hold back my orgasm.

"Oh, god, Gerald," Sanya moaned.

I gripped her thigh and lifted it over my hip, sinking deeper into her tight warmth. She bit her lip as I picked up the pace, thrusting hard and rocking the bed against the wall.

"Oh, fuck!" she whimpered, digging her nails into my back.

"No more running from me," I growled, kissing her slowly as we made love.

She moaned as I hovered over her. "No more running."

Chapter 4

Sanya

A *week later....*

"Crap!"

"What's wrong?" I questioned.

"My heel got caught in the drain, and now it's covered in dirt." Raya reached for a napkin to clean her shoe. She was one of the servers in the bar.

"Stop pouting. It'll be all right." I waved it off.

"Easy for you to say. I spent my last dime on these heels."

"Lord, you drive me crazy." I gestured to open up more packages of cigars.

"Anyway, why didn't you take that table?" Raya asked.

I hoped to avoid Gerald at all costs. "Because I'm not in the mood to deal with Gerald's attitude."

"Which one is Gerald?" She scanned the open floor plan of Billionaire Boys cigar bar and narrowed her eyes on the five men in suits laughing. They were all good-looking and sexy but probably assholes and playboys.

"Gerald's the one with the blond hair, goatee, and

light blue eyes." I wiped her glasses clean and opened another bottle of cognac to pour.

"We have to serve every table, Sanya. You can't pick and choose."

"I'm not interested in being around him right now." I sighed.

"Does he tip?"

"He tips very well. Are you coming to the book club this week?" I asked, changing the subject. My girls and I get together every month to read a new book that's captured our attention, and this week it's a thriller about JD. Robb released.

"Nice change of subject." Raya poked me in the side.

Gerald appeared, and we both froze.

His eyes narrowed on us. "What are you two up to?"

Raya cleared her throat but remained silent.

"Nothing. I was telling Raya to prepare the items for your table." I avoided eye contact with Gerald.

"I thought you were working at my table tonight," Gerald said.

"You did, but I had Shani change the schedule because I need to leave early," I answered, finally lifting my eyes to his.

"Leave early for what?" Gerald slipped his hands into his pockets.

"Gerald," I said warningly.

"Mr. Barlowe to you. Come to my office."

Our standoff was awkward, but I couldn't look away.

"Mr. Barlowe, we have tables waiting." I hissed, planting my hands on my hips.

"They can wait," Gerald fired back.

"Why? Because you're the owner?" I snapped.

My eyes widened as he closed the space between us. He was six-three, and his height intimidated most people, including me, when he was like this. When I was hired, I'd assumed that Troy was the owner, but boy, had I been wrong. There was no mistaking the stamp of authority Gerald had on this place.

"Raya, do you mind handling my table and letting my guests know I'll be out soon?" Gerald asked.

It was all I could do to keep my emotions in check. Usually, it didn't bother me when I worked at his table, but his nonchalant attitude pissed me off.

"Yes, Mr. Barlowe," Raya answered, picking up the drinks tray and turning to leave.

* * *

Grabbing my bags of groceries, I locked my car door and headed for my building. I dropped the bags at the sight that greeted me as I rounded the corner.

"Oh, my god." I rushed toward my building, which was surrounded by police and firefighters.

"I live here!" I shouted, trying to get through the crowd.

A police officer tried to calm me down. "Ma'am, we can't let you inside."

People were crying, and the building manager was talking with another policeman.

I yanked myself free and ran toward the ambulance. "Mr. Porter, what happened? I was gone for less than two hours."

Mr. Porter removed the blanket from around his

shoulders. "Not sure. They say it was electrical or something."

"Anyone hurt?"

"As far as I know, everybody is fine."

I moved toward the police tape, "Excuse me, officer. Can I go in to check on my apartment?"

"At this time, ma'am, we need everybody to stay back," he said, motioning for more officers to come to the front.

Hearing my phone ring, I snatched it from my purse, staring at what was left of my home. "Hello."

"Sanya?" Gerald's timing was impeccable.

"I can't talk right now." I was too distraught to get into a petty argument with him.

"What's wrong? Why do I hear sirens in the background?"

Tears welled. I felt defeated and had no choice but to let it all out. "My apartment building is on fire." I sobbed, dropping to the ground.

"Stay on the phone with me. I'm coming to you."

"You don't have to do that, Gerald. I'll be fine."

"No, you're not. Don't hang up this phone," he instructed.

I listened to him talk with his driver on the other end of the line, telling him to come to my address.

An hour later, I sat on his couch in his condo. I was wearing his shirt, covered in a blanket, and drinking tea while the news reported the incident at my building.

Gerald stood at the dining room table with food he had his chef prepare. "You need to eat."

"I'm not hungry."

"Baby, you need to eat and build your strength."

"I have to find a place to stay. I only have about two thousand saved." I groaned in frustration at my situation.

"You don't need to find a new place. You can stay here."

I stared at him. "What did you say?"

"I said you can stay here."

"Gerald, we barely know each other."

"That's a lie."

"Yes, we've fucked, but you know what I mean."

"Stop placing these conditions on us, Sanya. Time has no bearing on what we are to each other."

"You're thirty-nine, single, and a billionaire. I'm twenty-eight. How do I know you won't wake up one day and want something different? I want a career and a family and kids."

"Have I given you a reason to think I don't want any of that?"

"That's because our time together is always on your terms," I pointed out.

"What do you want, Sanya?"

"I-I need you to understand that I refuse to be a trophy girlfriend."

"Staying with me is the only logical thing, plus I need you as my date."

"Date for what?"

"Remington's charity event."

"When is it?"

He walked toward his home office. "In a week."

"A week!" I hopped off the couch to follow him. He removed his jacket and sat in his chair, ignoring my frown.

"Have Melinda take you shopping to get what you need."

"I didn't agree to stay here."

"We both know you have no choice."

"Wanna bet?"

"Staying with Melinda is out of the question. Her fiancé wouldn't go for it, and your parents live in another state." Gerald listed off my choices, and he was right.

"Fuck you." I slammed my hand on his desk and stomped out of his office.

"We can do that after we get your things moved in here," Gerald called out.

"I hate you!" I screamed, slamming the guest bedroom door.

Chapter 5

Gerald

I rode in the back of my limo, listening to Melinda run through my schedule. I had twenty minutes to get to my appointment. I scheduled my meetings today and hated leaving Sanya after our heated argument last night. The way her body melted when she let me hold her in my arms put me in a different mindset, and I needed to make her understand that I wasn't playing games.

Opening another club in a new location was the goal of the day. Douglas, my driver, parked out front, I hopped out of the limo as Melinda gathered her things, and Douglas helped her from the other side. I looked up at the building we were considering for the new club. It was two stories and was located in the heart of Manhattan. I opened the door for Melinda, scanning the interior.

"Mr. Barlowe, thank you for coming." The realtor, Shanice, held her hand out to me.

"I came because you told me this place was worth my time, Shanice."

Shanice was beautiful, but she acted like I should

want her just because of her looks. Women impressed me when they had personality, drive, dreams, and beauty. Shanice was the type to flirt with me one minute and fuck someone else the next.

"I promise you will fall in love," Shanice assured me, handing me the brochure with all the information.

Melinda looked annoyed with Shanice, and I couldn't blame her. Shanice is more interested in sleeping with me than selling property.

Melinda pushed her glasses up her nose. "Can you tell us about the building, or is that above your pay grade?"

Shanice rolled her eyes before giving us a tour of the lounge area. Feeling my phone vibrate, a message came through with a picture of Sanya talking with another man. I strained to get a better look, my eyes squinted in confusion, and my nostrils flared in agitation. Simon Butler was at my club in Sanya's presence.

"Send the information to my office. We need to cut this short." I turned and walked away, with Melinda scurrying to keep up.

"What's going on?" Melinda asked breathlessly.

I held up my phone to show her the picture.

"Gerald, it could be innocent."

"He's in my club talking to my woman."

Rubbing her forehead in annoyance. "So you two are officially a couple?"

"Yes."

Melinda tilted her head. "Does she know that?"

"She knows."

"Simon's an ass. He's not worth your time."

"He knows not to go to my place."

"I thought he was banned?"

"He is. I guess he figured my not being there gave him a pass. I saw Remington in the background."

"Try not to make a scene."

"Not going to happen."

Douglas sped back to the club. Sanya avoiding me since our night together pissed me off even more.

"Douglas, run the red light if you have to," I instructed.

Melinda frowned. "Douglas, ignore him."

Douglas chuckled. I appreciated Melinda for not being intimidated.

* * *

When Douglas parked, I jumped out and headed inside with Melinda hot on my heels. I spotted Simon, and she stood between us as I reached out to pull him from his seat. "Get out of my club."

"Gerald, you continue to display a pattern of behavior. Still jealous of the money and women I have?" Simon chortled, putting down his cigar.

"Yo, G. Not here," Remington pleaded.

"He needs to leave," I snapped.

"Why? I like the service here." Simon reached into his pocket, pulled out cash, and placed it on the bar top.

Sanya covered my hand. "Gerald, relax. It's just a drink."

"He's banned."

"Mr. Barlowe," Melinda said.

I raised a hand for everybody to shut up. "Simon, you have three seconds to leave, or security will toss your cocky ass out of here."

He slowly rose from the stool and winked at Sanya.

The gesture sent me into a different realm. I lunged at him, and Remington held me back. Simon laughed as he sauntered from the club.

Sanya slammed the bottle on the counter and marched to the back.

"Wait! Give her some space," Melinda said as I started to follow her.

"I'll fucking kill him."

"No, you won't. Have a drink with me," Remington said.

Chapter 6

Sanya

I ignored Gerald's calls and texts after he embarrassed me with his possessiveness in front of everyone. He'd demanded I stay at his condo, telling me he'd stay at his main home.

The girls were going out tonight, and I promised to tag along to hang out and get a break from work. I washed and dried my hair and put on a little makeup. Gathering my things, I headed outside, where my ride was waiting. I planned on asking Raya or Melinda if I could crash with them so I could move on from the fights with Gerald.

Hopping into the car, I gave the driver directions to the club. I sat back, thinking about how much my life had changed from a year ago. When I left college with a business degree, there weren't many jobs for women. Working as a bottle girl led me to Billionaire Boys Club, and the money that came with it was way better than any nine-to-five. Learning the landscape of a club and gaining the trust and knowledge of the customer's needs gave me insight into how to move forward with my business.

My ride pulled up outside, and I paid the driver, adding a tip.

Exiting the car, I sauntered up to the doorman. "I'm meeting some friends."

"Go ahead, sexy." The doorman licked his lips. "Come talk to me when you leave," he called after me.

"No thanks." I scanned the crowd, seeing that Melinda had a booth already for us. Someone grabbed my hand as I pushed through the people, and I froze.

"Sexy Sanya," Simon murmured.

I looked down at my hand and back at him. "Simon."

"Come have a drink with me."

Simon wasn't bad looking. He was a few inches shorter than Gerald at five-nine, with short spiky black hair, dark brown eyes, and muscular arms, but with a little weight around his stomach. "No, thank you."

"Are you worried Gerald might catch us?"

"Gerald is not my husband."

"Glad to know."

I raised an eyebrow. "Why?"

"Makes the chase easier."

"Not interested in, Simon. Please stop trying to make Gerald jealous."

"One drink." He held up his index finger.

"Sorry, my girls are waiting." I strolled to the closed-off section in the corner of the back room.

I hugged Melinda, Raya, and Stacy and sat down to grab a drink.

"Who was that?" Stacy asked.

"Nobody."

"Simon's asking for trouble," Melinda said.

Stacy twisted in her seat. "Please, tell me how you catch them, girl. He's fine."

I ignored her comment and clinked glasses with Raya before taking a swig of my martini.

"No men talk for the night. We're here to have fun." Melinda stood, swaying her hips to the music.

"Let's get fucking wasted." Raya joked as Melinda twerked against the wall. "She's too much." Raya turned to look at me. "Can I ask you something?"

"Sure."

"So this guy asked me out."

"Really?"

She nodded and sighed. "I'm not sure how to feel about it."

"What's the event?

"A charity event, and it would be around some very important people," Raya replied.

"Raya, you're gorgeous, and any man would be lucky to have you."

"Maybe, but I'm nervous."

"When's the event?"

"In two days."

"And you are just now telling me?"

"Shush...You know that being around all these high society folks is new to me."

"Raya, whoever gets to be beside you is a lucky man. Tomorrow, we'll go shopping for a dress."

"Do you think I should go?"

"Hell, yes!" Melinda screamed, bumping butts with Stacy.

Shaking my head at the girls, Raya and I joined in and let the other stress go for now.

* * *

Melinda said it was fine for me to crash at her place until my apartment was livable again. We were still hungover when we met Raya at the mall the next day. Rifling through the racks at Bergdorf Goodman, we picked out about ten gowns between us for her to try on.

"Remind me never to go out with you guys and drink that much again," Melinda groaned as we sat outside Raya's changing room.

I laughed. "We warned you about overdoing it, but you wanted to live it up."

"Yeah, yeah." Melinda stuck her tongue out at me.

"Have you talked to Gerald?" I passed another dress to Raya to try on.

"Why are you asking about Gerald? I thought he didn't factor into your life.

"He doesn't." My cheeks heated at my lie.

"Lie to him, not us." Melinda teased.

"Focus on your fiancé, and leave me alone."

Melinda smirked as her phone rang, interrupting us. "Hey, boss." She put the phone on speaker.

"Is Sanya next to you?" Gerald asked.

I waved my hands in her face and mouthed, "No."

"No, boss," Melinda answered.

"I don't appreciate you lying to me." Gerald didn't wait for a reply and ended the call.

I sighed. "He's lost his mind."

"Then help me find it."

I froze at the deep voice behind me. I turned slowly to see Gerald with a stern expression. "What are you doing here?"

"We need to talk."

"I'm busy."

"Sanya, you know I'm capable of shutting this place

down. Are you ready for me to show my strength?" Gerald demanded.

"Go ahead, Sanya. We'll catch up with you later," Melinda urged.

I glared at her. "Traitor."

Raya came out in her dress and looked from Gerald to me.

I huffed. "It's a long story."

I left the girls to drive home with Gerald. The way he took charge made my panties wet, but I would never confess that to him.

Chapter 7

Gerald

Sanya's eyes stayed glued to the phone in her hand while driving to the senator's event. Hearing that Simon had tried to get close to Sanya only made me more determined to show Sanya what she and I could have if we stopped fighting our feelings.

I ran my hand up her thigh, but she removed it and crossed her legs. Douglas parked the limo outside the Biltmore Hotel, and the valet opened the door and helped Sanya out.

Grasping her hand, I hugged her close and kissed her cheek. "Stop fighting me."

"No."

"Play nice, or we can do it the hard way."

"After tonight, I'm going to stay with Melinda."

"No, you're not." I waved to the cameras. "Smile for the cameras."

"So you want me to fake it."

"If you like."

"Simon's right about you."

"Keep pissing me off, Sanya, and see what happens."

The doorman ushered us inside. I looked around the space in awe of what Remington had accomplished. This charity event meant a lot to him, and I was happy to come and show my support. Noticing him talking and laughing with his parents, I walked over with Sanya.

"Champagne, beautiful?" Simon appeared in front of us, holding out a glass.

"Take your champagne and shove it up your ass," I growled.

I hated to cause an issue at Remington's event, but Simon was becoming a real problem. I blocked his view of Sanya, forcing her behind me and taking the champagne glass from his hand. I snagged a passing waiter and placed the glass on the tray. "She doesn't need anything from you."

"Gerald, you're embarrassing me." Sanya clenched her teeth.

"Sanya, I'd expect you to be with a classier gentleman," Simon taunted.

"Simon, please, don't."

"Don't speak to her," I warned.

"Says who?" Simon closed the space between us, and Sanya placed her hand on my chest to hold me back.

The waiter sensed the tension and beat a hasty retreat.

"Simon, I've told you I'm not interested in you," Sanya snapped.

She took my hand and led me away. I kissed the back of her hand, but Sanya still avoided talking to me.

"Can't stay mad all night."

"You'd be surprised."

We greeted Remington and his family, and Sanya

hugged Remington. I shook hands with Remington and his father and kissed his mother on the cheek.

"I see you and Simon aren't getting along," Remington observed.

"Gerald, who is the lovely lady on your arm tonight," Mrs. Ayton, Remington's mother, asked.

"Mrs. Ayton, I'd like you to meet my date, Sanya. She works for me."

"Hello." Sanya smiled, shaking hands with Mrs. Ayton.

"Honey, you're gorgeous," Mrs. Ayton said.

Sanya giggled as Mr. Ayton kissed her knuckles. "Nice to meet you, Mr. Ayton."

"Mr. Ayton, you're holding onto my woman's hand a little too long," I teased.

"Son, if you haven't married this one yet, you're doing it all wrong." He chuckled, and Mrs. Ayton joined in on the joke. It irritated me to hear Sanya and Remington laughing.

The announcer introduced Remington, who was giving a speech. Sanya stood in front of me with her back to my chest.

I planted my hands on her waist, muzzling my nose in her hair. "All that laughing was uncalled for."

Her laughter vibrated through my chest. "I like when you're laid back and less grumpy."

"I like when you're all mine."

She swiveled to face me, placing her hands on my chest. "Simon is not my type."

I grazed my finger over her nose. "Glad you know that."

"Stop being mean."

"Stop being beautiful. Have you thought about my offer?"

"Yes, and I have some rules."

"Rules?"

"Yes, before I agree. We have to keep it professional."

"No."

She dropped her hands to her hips, "I'm serious, Gerald. If I take the position, you can't play favorites or expect me to be at your beck and call."

"Says who?"

"Me. I want the girls to know I got the job because I have the skills."

I eyed her curvy body, "You've got the skills."

Sanya slapped my chest. "Skills beyond the bedroom, sir."

I kissed the top of her head. "Baby, the only opinion that matters is mine. If anyone has a problem with that, they'll get fired."

"Firing them because they talk about me isn't right."

"If someone is fucking with you, they should be grateful I only fire them."

We walked to the designated tables, and I pulled out her chair as the crowd applauded Remington's speech.

The food arrived, and I watched Sanya indulge, wondering how it would be working alongside her at my club.

Sanya moaned as she tasted her food.

"I could eat you right now," I said gruffly.

She sipped her drink. "Dessert is coming out soon."

"I'd rather have you for dessert."

She smirked. "I bet you would."

* * *

Throwing the door open, I lifted Sanya in my arms, and she wrapped her legs around my waist. She cupped my face, capturing my lips, and her moan made my dick even harder. I planned to devour every smooth curve of her body with my tongue, hands, and dick.

I carried her to my room and set her on her feet. She held onto me for balance as I removed her shoes and unzipped her dress, letting it fall to the floor.

I took her in, and she shivered under my gaze. I wanted to prolong the anticipation. I wanted her to know I would take her body to new heights.

"Sanya, I want you to understand what I'm about to do."

"What are you about to do, sir?"

I smirked. "Sir?"

I bent to remove her thong and placed it in my pocket.

"Stop teasing me, sir."

I caressed her breasts, tweaking her nipples. "You are so fucking sexy."

Her head fell back, and she moaned. "Keep going."

Chapter 8

Sanya

I knew I wouldn't stay mad at Gerald for long. His warmth and compassion were things I'd craved in a partner. Knowing he would protect me but still respect my boundaries and trust me to stand on my own.

"Gerald," I whimpered as his hand moved between my thighs and his finger glided across my slit.

"So warm and ready for me, baby."

Squeezing my eyes tight, my hips started to move in rhythm with his finger. He lifted his finger to my breast and swirled my essence around my nipple. I gasped, and my eyes fluttered shut as he lowered his head and sucked the tender bud into his mouth.

He wrapped his other hand around my neck. "Keep your eyes open, baby."

My conscience told me not to get involved with my boss and that it would lead to disaster, but Gerald had a hold on me.

"Take off your clothes, please."

I watched as he removed his clothes. I wanted him with a ferocity that shocked me. I loved having him inside me, the rawness of his movements, and the peace he brought me. The bed dipped as we fell on it. I spread my legs, and his grin told me our night would be long. He kissed a path from my ankle to my inner thighs, rubbing his face against my pussy. I arched my back on the bed, trying to hold in my moans as my legs trembled.

"God, you're beautiful when you come for me," he growled against my sensitive flesh. "You ready for me, baby?"

I reached for his dick and lined it up with my entrance. "Please."

Gerald wasn't the only possessive one in this relationship. No other woman would ever experience this because he belonged to me.

He surged inside me, and my heightened emotions had me racing toward my orgasm.

"I'm coming, baby!" I cried.

He moved faster, groaning at hearing his pleasure in my ear. "Fuck, Sanya. Love seeing you come, baby."

He collapsed against me before rolling onto his side, pulling me with him. I rested my head on his chest as our breathing slowly returned to normal. For the first time, I felt like I meant something to Gerald.

* * *

The weekend arrived, and Simon invited me to lunch. I wanted to decline, but he insisted it was purely business and would help build my clientele.

Simon walked up to the table and sat across from me. "Sanya, you look lovely today."

"Thanks. So what's this business you wanted to talk about?"

"I have a proposal for you, but I want to eat first."

"Simon, please understand this meeting is business, nothing more."

"What do you want out of life, Sanya?"

"Why do you ask?"

Our waitress came to the table to fill our water glasses, and we gave our orders. Sitting back in my chair, I waited for Simon to continue.

He removed his shades and tossed them onto the table, reaching out to cover my hand with his. "I think we'd be good together."

I snatched my hand away and stood to leave.

Simon jumped up and grabbed my arm. "Wait, Sanya. Listen to me."

"There's nothing for us to talk about."

"I see the potential in you, Sanya, and working for my company could lead to bigger things."

I raised my eyebrow. "Like what?"

"Money, fame, status."

"I have money."

"But do you have the backing and status? As my assistant, you would have access to the most influential people in entertainment, politics, and much more."

"Gerald already offered me a job."

"Working for his little club? Please."

"I like working at the club."

"But can you travel the world and rub shoulders with high society?"

"I've never been the type to be around high society."

The server brought our food. I thanked her and listened as Simon continued his pitch.

"Just imagine it. Europe, Asia, and Australia. Meeting with presidents, senators, and celebrities."

"Sounds good, but I need to think it over."

"Why think about an opportunity I'm throwing on the table for free."

"Would you want something in return?"

"Something beyond our friendship? I won't lie. You're a very beautiful woman, Sanya. I'd be an idiot not to pursue you."

"Gerald offered me a job and told you to stay away from me."

"Is Gerald your husband?"

"No, of course not."

"Okay. So, please hear me out before you decide."

My phone rang, and I glanced at the screen to see Melinda's name. I let it go to voicemail and ordered another bottle of wine.

Chapter 9

Gerald

When Sanya didn't answer my call, I had Melinda find out where she'd gone.

The hostess approached me as I stalked into the restaurant. She scanned the guest list in her hand worriedly. "Hello, Mr. Barlowe. We don't seem to have a reservation for you, but—"

"I see who I'm here for," I cut across her.

My eyes narrow on Sanya as she throws her head back in laughter, highlighting the long neck I loved to trace with my tongue.

Simon's dumb ass didn't faze me, but he'd overstepped too many times, and I was ready to put an end to his bullshit.

Sanya looked up in surprise as I came to a halt by their table. "Gerald! What are you doing here?"

"I could ask you the same thing."

"Simon and I are talking business."

Simon interjected. "Gerald, you know Sanya is an extremely intelligent woman. I understand you offered her a new role at your little club, but I have bigger plans for her."

Simon's smug grin made me seethe. "If you want to finish the meal on your plate, you need to shut your mouth."

"Don't embarrass me, please," Sanya hissed, peering around the restaurant to ensure no one was watching.

"Time to go," I barked at her.

"I'm not leaving," Sanya muttered.

Simon sat forward in his chair and tried to grab Sanya's hand. "Listen to the lady. She wants to be here."

Sanya squealed in shock as I lunged at Simon and pressed his head to the table.

"Gerald, let him go," Sanya demanded as other diners videoed the scene.

"Get your hands off me! Call the police!" Simon shouted.

I bent close to his ear. "This is your final warning. If you make one more attempt to talk to her, I'll kill you." Releasing him, I fixed my jacket and held out my hand to Sanya.

"That was unnecessary." Sanya threw her napkin on the table, snatched up her purse, and marched out of the restaurant.

Taking out my wallet, I placed a hundred dollars on the table. "That's to cover her meal and a tip." His furious gaze told me how much he wanted to retaliate, but he remained seated. I patted his shoulder. "Wise choice."

I turned and left the restaurant, catching up with Sanya before she could get in her car. I plucked her keys from her hand and stood in front of the driver's door.

"Move, Mr. Barlowe," she gritted.

"Oh, I'm back to being Mr. Barlowe now?"

"You know that was uncalled for. You behaved like a child."

I buried my head in her neck, "Fuck Simon."

"We both know I would never be with Simon, so why are you acting like a possessive, over-the-top asshole?"

"Because it's your fault."

"How?"

"Baby, you might not understand, but you're everything to me. The minute anyone else sees what I see, I get crazy. I love you."

Her eyes widen. "Love me?"

"I was fooling myself, but I've been in love with you since you walked into my office."

She looped her arms around my neck and pressed her lips to mine. "Gerald Barlowe, I love you too."

I drop my forehead to hers. "Finally."

She smiles. "Let's go home."

* * *

Once I let Simon know Sanya was off limits, he hadn't contacted her again. I promised Sanya we'd make things official at the club, so I'd gathered the staff to announce our relationship. Holding the meeting on a Sunday made sense since we were closed. Cariss stood in the corner gossiping with her usual group of girls like they were in high school.

"Ladies, gather around," I instructed.

Some remained standing while others sat.

"Gerald, why are we here?" Cariss demanded.

"It's Mr. Barlowe to you," Sanya snapped.

I shook my head at Sanya, but she shrugged. I grasped her hand, and Cariss gasped. The murmurs grew louder as the employees looked between Sanya and me in shock.

"I know I have a rule about dating coworkers," I began.

"So what the fuck is this?" Cariss pointed at us.

"Keep giving him attitude, and you're going to regret it, little girl," Sanya barked.

"Girl, please." Cariss waved her off.

"Behave, Cariss, or find another job," I said, holding her gaze.

"Mr. Barlowe and I are dating. Well, we're together," Sanya announced.

"For how long?" another employee questioned.

"A few months."

"All you need to know is that Sanya is going to manage the club moving forward, and no, she didn't get the position because we're together," I said clearly.

"I assure you my goal is not to come in and take over, and there will be no favoritism," Sanya explained.

"Oh, please," Cariss said, addressing the other employees.

"Cariss, if you have something to say, by all means, let us know," Sanya challenged, already stepping up to the plate as the boss.

Cariss rolled her eyes. "I have nothing to say."

"As usual," Sanya snipped.

"Now that we're clear, enjoy the rest of your day." I took Sanya by the hand and dragged her to my office, shutting the door behind us.

"I wasn't finished." She pouted.

My lips crashed against hers, "Baby, my dick is hard right now, and I need to be inside you."

Sanya reached into my pants and took out my dick.

She dropped to her knees and took me in her warm mouth, swirling her tongue around my engorged crown. I let her tease me for a few minutes until I couldn't take anymore. Needing to be inside her, I pulled her off my hard length and helped her to stand.

"Come sit on my face," I teased.

She smirked. "Where it all began."

Sanya lay on the couch and spread her legs. Taking her sweet pussy and hearing her cries of pleasure was all I needed for the rest of my life.

Chapter 10

Gerald

A month later

Every day, I became more aware of how much Sanya had control of my every emotion. I watched as she prepared the staff to open for the day, feeling like a proud boyfriend—hell, even a potential husband. A man who was finally ready to admit his feelings for the woman who made his world better.

Chugging back the scotch, I admired her ass jiggle as she walked around the room, ensuring we had the tables set with the correct items.

I pressed the button to close the viewing panel between my office and the bar and moved back to my desk.

Remington entered with a gloomy look and marched over to the bar in the corner. "I need to find a new job."

Laughing, I waited for him to pour a second glass and sit opposite me. "Problems at work?"

"Simon reached out to me."

"Simon thinks you can talk me into leaving him alone."

Remington arched an eyebrow, "He's not after Sanya anymore."

"I know."

"Then why are you putting dirt on his name?"

Simon had kept his word and stopped pursuing Sanya, but I still cut into deals he tried to make with important people. It reminded me daily how much pull I had in the city. "Because I can."

Remington groaned and rubbed the back of his neck. "Really, G?"

"He started it. I told him I'd be the one to finish it."

"I hear you, but it's time to move on. You got the girl, and she's happy with you."

I sipped my drink, whirling the ice around with my finger. "When did you talk to him?"

"At a business meeting on re-election plans."

"You look like shit."

"I'm exhausted. I need to hire a new assistant."

"Sanya might be able to find someone for you."

"Thanks, but I need you to back off Simon until I can get him on board with my re-election plans."

"I can cut you a check right now. Going through him will make you one of his flunkies."

"Simon's not stupid. He's an important asset in the political arena."

My office swung open, and Sanya entered, holding some documents. She leaned in and kissed me as she reached my desk. "Hey, Mr. Barlowe."

"What did I tell you about calling me Mr. Barlowe?"

"Sorry, baby." She grinned. "Hi, Senator Ayton."

Remington held up his hands in mock annoyance. "Come on, Sanya. Not me, too."

Giggling, Sanya shook her head. "Gerald hates when I call him by his last name."

"You on a break?" I asked.

"In ten minutes. I came to bring you the forms about the new building inspection."

I tossed them in the pile of things I needed to read over when I had time.

"G, I'll call you later, and we can discuss that matter further," Remington said.

"My mind's made up."

"What matter?" Sanya inquired.

I glared at Remington, daring him to reveal what we'd discussed about Simon.

He smirked as he downed his drink and spilled to Sanya like a kid tattling to his mom. "Your boy is fucking with Simon."

Sanya's eyes whipped to mine. "Is that true?"

My blood pressure rose. "Fuck Simon."

"I told you I was never interested in Simon. Please stop bothering him."

"Why? Sounds like you're trying to spare his ass."

"I'm out, man. Sanya, don't be too hard on him." Remington winked as he left my office.

I wanted to kick his ass for starting shit with my girl. Reaching an arm around her waist, I pulled her onto my lap.

She narrowed her eyes on me. "Be nice to Simon."

"No."

"You're behaving like a little boy, not the grown man fell in love with."

Brushing a finger over her bottom lip, I pressed a kiss to her chin. "You love me, yes?"

She sighed and wrapped her arms around my neck. "Yes, even when you're acting like an ass."

I kissed her, nibbling her bottom lip and sliding my tongue into her mouth.

Sanya pulled back reluctantly. "I have to get back to work."

"I'll leave the bastard alone," I relented.

"Thank you. I need another favor."

"What?"

"Can we have the book club at your condo?" Sanya pleaded, putting her hands in a prayer position.

"First my club, and now my condo? You and Melinda need more friends."

Sanya burst into laughter as she stood to leave. "How about I cook dinner for us at your place tonight?"

"Dinner at *our* place," I corrected.

She smiled. "Our place."

"Then you and I will have a little conversation about how your book club is ruining my life."

"My book club has made your life better, buddy."

I grunted in reply, adjusting my hard dick as she sashayed from my office. My woman was going to drive me crazy.

Epilogue

Sanya

Six months later

I lounged in the hammock on the patio of the beach house, watching the waves rumble in and out. I couldn't remember the last time I'd felt this relaxed.

Finally lowering my guard and committing to Gerald was a blessing, and he'd lived up to his promise about me managing the club. Neither of us wanted a relationship in the beginning, but we were incredibly happy now.

"Thank you for the invite," Raya said, plucking a frozen drink from the tray the server brought with a murmured thanks.

I made a mental note to check that the chef had prepared Gerald's favorite dessert after dinner.

"Stop thanking me. You've been a blessing as a friend."

Raya turned to face me. "Any plans for your next trip?"

I sat up in excitement, ready to spill my surprise. I checked the beach to ensure no one was close by. "Gerald has no clue I scheduled his private jet to take us to Dubai for his birthday.”

“Dubai is amazing.”

“I’m ready to spend a week alone with him.”

Turning forty was a milestone, and I hoped for the best year for him and us as a couple. Stepping into his cigar bar a year ago had led to my dreams coming true.

Raya held her glass up, and we toasted.

“Sanya, can you come up to the house and help me find my watch?” Gerald appeared beside me under the cabana, blocking the son.

Pushing my shades down, I scanned his wrist and saw the brand-new Rolex. “What’s that?”

Gerald glanced at his wrist and shrugged. He bent and plucked me from the hammock.

“Gerald!” I screeched.

Raya laughed as she videoed us on her phone.

“Shush.” Gerald pecked me on the lips.

I wrapped my legs around his waist as he carried me to the house and into our room, kicking the door shut behind him. He lowered me to the bed, eyeing my one-piece bathing suit.

“You’re dangerous, Mr. Barlowe.”

“You like danger, baby.” Gerald hovered over me on the bed.

“Only with you.”

“Good answer.”

“What about our guests?”

He dropped his shorts and covered my body with his, kissing along my shoulder up my neck. “I have a surprise.”

“A surprise?”

Nodding, he pulled back and for his discarded shorts,

removing a small box. My heart hammered as he bent to kiss me. "I know about Dubai."

"How?" I pouted.

"Baby, I know everything. My team keeps me updated whenever my schedule changes."

I sighed in frustration. "I wanted to surprise you."

He slid the box open. "Well, why don't you surprise me by doing me the honor of becoming my wife."

My hands flew to my cheeks, and my eyes brimmed with tears. I scanned his face before looking at the oval-shaped diamond ring. I nodded. "Yes."

"Yes?"

"Yes," I confirmed.

I held out my hand, and he slipped the ring on my finger before smashing his lips to mine.

"I love you so much, Gerald."

"Baby, you've made me the happiest man in the world." Gerald slipped his hand inside my bikini bottoms, pushing a finger inside me.

I let out a breath. "Baby."

"This is why I go crazy over you," he growled.

We made out for the rest of the day as we consummated our engagement and the day I became a part of his world at Billionaire Boys Club.

* * *

I hope you enjoyed Sanya and Gerald's story. Check out the next book in the series, **"Promise Me,"** a forbidden, age gap romance https://books2read.com/u/mB5nRA

Have you checked out **"His Peace Her Plea-sure?"** Click here:

https://books2read.com/u/3JJr0P, a billionaire, steamy romance.

Also, steamy romance that includes bodyguard, one-night stands, and marital issues tropes: ***"Seeking In Romance 1-6."***

https://books2read.com/u/4ELGLe

Don't forget if you love Fling romances, bodyguard, and forced proximity, check out **"Protecting Chanel"** https://books2read.com/u/mqwPB8

If you love brother's best friend romance, then you'll love **"Sensual"** here:

https://books2read.com/u/49lYYM with a dash of steamy romance.

Check out Bodyguard Romance, military, romantic suspense here ***"Protecting Bria."***

https://books2read.com/u/bQJkjd

Follow college romance and more characters in ***"Taste"*** here:

https://books2read.com/u/bpz1Ng

How about a steamy, medical romance? Check out ***"Haven."***

https://books2read.com/u/4jAvyZ a steamy, enemies-to-lovers romance.

Please also check out my ***"Love Don't Live Here Anymore Vanessa Andrew."***

https://books2read.com/u/mBOWGZ a steamy curvy girl, enemies to lovers romance.

Follow that up with a workplace vacation romance in **"Love Don't Live Here Anymore Isabella Andrew."**

https://books2read.com/u/brVNO7

More workplace, boss romances with **"Love by Design Boxset 1-3."**
https://books2read.com/u/m2ldEk

Sneak Peek: Promise Me

Can I have power and love, or will one ruin the other?

During the day I am a Senator.

A man of power and expectations set for me.

But at night, there is one place I can unwind and just be me.

Raya was supposed to be a distraction from the politics and the pressures of my life.

Instead, she becomes an addiction. A force so seductive and sweet, I fall for her instantly.

I want to promise her a lifetime of love, but dating outside the boundaries threatens to destroy our love.

Will this forbidden romance endure, or will my career leave me hurt and alone?

Indulge in seduction in this new series from KeKe Renée. During the day these billionaires are powerful tycoons that run the city, but at night, they come to Billionaire Boy's Club play.

About the Author

A TENNESSEE NATIVE, and California dreaming Author KeKe Renée is living and striving to continue her passion of writing short story romances in genres ranging from Erotic, Paranormal, and Women's Fiction.

Catalog of Releases By Keke Renée:

•Wet Heat (Wet Heat Series Book 1)

•Every Time We Touch Novelette (Wet Heat Book 2 Series)

•His Peace, Her Pleasure

•Baby, It's Cold Outside

•Love Don't Live Here Anymore, Vanessa Andrew Book 1

•Love Don't Live Here Anymore, Isabella Andrew Book 2

•One Night Only—A Novelette (Love by Design Book 1)

•Cassian and Savannah (Love by Design Book 2)

•Deidra's Love (Love by Design Book 3)

•Protecting Bria (Special Force Operation Alphas)

Thank you so much for reading. `if you enjoyed the crazy ride and decide to leave a review, we'd truly appreciate the support.

What's Next

WANT TO KNOW WHAT HAPPENS next?

Follow me on Bookbub and social media today.

Reviews are the lifeblood of the publishing world. They're read, appreciated, and needed. Please consider taking the time to leave a few words wherever you buy books. Sign up for updates and sneak peeks at the site below.

304 Publishing Company

WE SHOWCASE AUTHORS writing African American, Interracial, Women's Fiction, Urban Romance, Erotic, and Contemporary Romance novels. Along with Thriller, Suspense, Poetry, Beauty, and Style Books. Thank you for taking the time to visit. Join our mailing list to stay updated with new releases and blog posts.